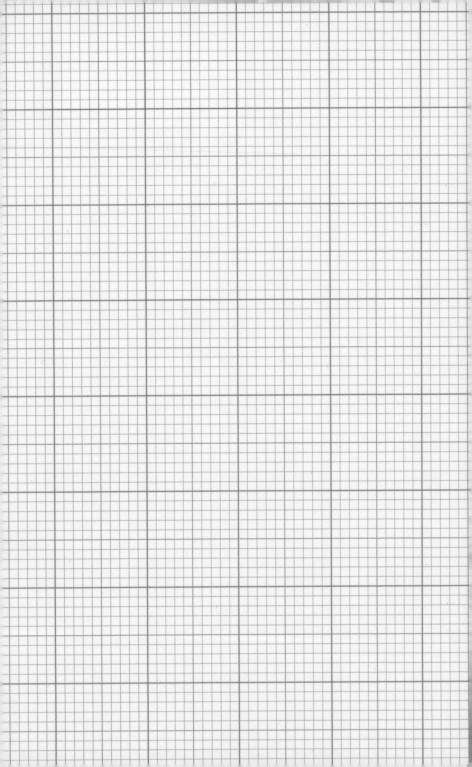

THIS NOTEBOOK BELONGS TO:

ROSie

THE QUESTIONEERS

ROSIE REVERE

AND THE RAUCOUS RIVETERS

by Andrea Beaty   illustrated by David Roberts

AMULET BOOKS

NEW YORK

Library of Congress Cataloging-in-Publication Data
Names: Beaty, Andrea, author. | Roberts, David, 1970- illustrator. Title: Rosie Revere and the Raucous Riveters / by Andrea Beaty; illustrated by David Roberts. Description: New York: Amulet Books, 2018. | Summary: When Rosie is unable to invent a contraption to help one of Aunt Rose's Raucous Riveters friends, she calls on classmates Iggy Peck and Ada Twist to help. Identifiers: LCCN 2018009612 | ISBN 9781419733604 (hardcover pob) Subjects: | CYAC: Engineers—Fiction. | Inventions—Fiction | Failure (Psychology)—Fiction. | Perseverance (Ethics)—Fiction. Classification: LCC PZ7.B380547 Ros 2018 | DDC [E]—dc23

ABRAMS The Art of Books
195 Broadway, New York, NY 10007
abramsbooks.com

FOR ANNa and Alexandra,
I love you.
—A. B.

FOR Chad W. BECKERMAN.
—D. R.

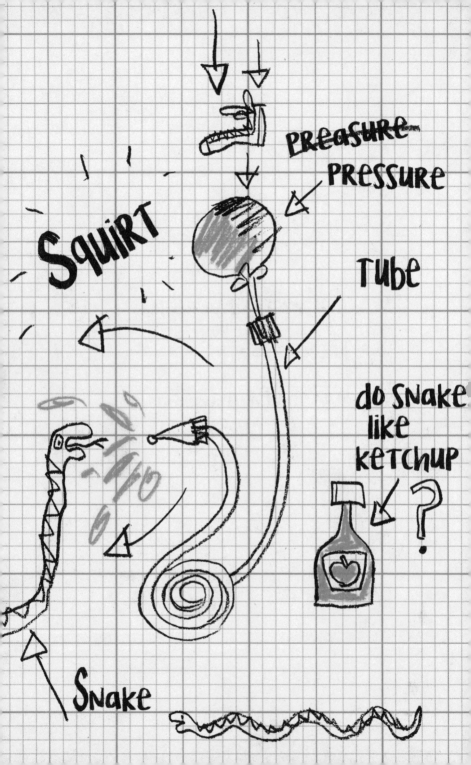

CHAPTER 1

Rosie Revere put on her safety goggles.

"Are you ready?" she asked.

"Ready!" said Ada Twist.

"Ready!" said Iggy Peck.

They signaled the thumbs-up from behind the kitchen counter.

"Here goes!" said Rosie.

She hit the big red button on the Count-o-meter. A scratchy computer voice blared from its speaker.

COUNTDOWN!

FIVE . . .

Rosie ducked into her safety booth.

FOUR . . .

She flipped open her notebook.

THREE . . .

She pulled her pencil from behind her ear.

TWO . . .

Suddenly, Gizmo flew into the kitchen and landed on the contraption.

"DUCK!" yelled Rosie.

Gizmo chirped angrily.

"I know you're not a duck!" yelled Rosie.

ONE . . .

The three kids dived for Gizmo just as—

BOOM!

The contraption exploded.

SPLAT! SPLOP! SPLURP!

Sticky, red glops of ketchup flew everywhere! But Gizmo zoomed ahead of the storm. She soared up, up, and out of the way. She looped the loop and gently landed on the refrigerator.

"Zowie!" said Ada, wiping ketchup from her goggles.

"Yikes!" said Iggy, wiping ketchup from his sweater.

"Hmm," said Rosie, tapping her pencil on her notebook.

Rosie looked at the mess and wrote a quick note:

TESTING IN KITCHEN = Bad idea!

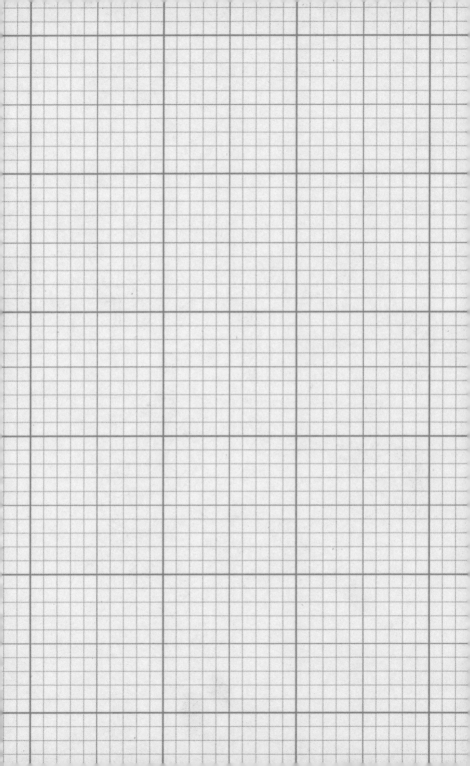

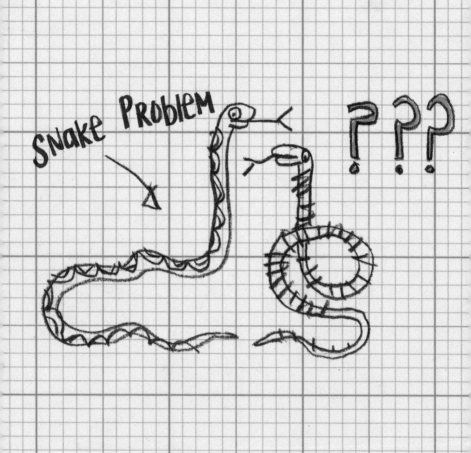

CHAPTER 2

Ada and Iggy had been helping Rosie all morning. She was trying to invent something for her uncle, Zookeeper Fred. Uncle Fred had a big-snake problem . . . and a little-snake problem . . . and a green-snake problem . . . and a . . .

Uncle Fred had an EVERY-kind-of-snake problem. Every kind of snake in the zoo loved him.

They slithered out of the cages and into his office. They hid in his desk. In his pockets. Even

in his lunch! One day, a smooth green snake named Vern hid in his sandwich. Uncle Fred thought that Vern was a wiggly pickle and almost took a bite!

After that, Uncle Fred called Rosie. She invented a contraption to scare away snakes. She called it the SnakeAway. It failed. She tried again. And again. And again. Rosie invented five models. They all failed, but she did not give up. Uncle Fred needed her help.

Rosie had hoped that the SnakeAway Model 5 would do the job. She looked at the mess. The fake snake on the table was covered in ketchup. It looked like a gigantic striped french fry with fangs. Uncle Fred would not like an invention that left ketchup all over his desk. He was a mustard kind of guy. And besides, it might attract ants. And possibly french fries.

Rosie added some notes about her testing:

Model 1: Fabulous Flop
Model 2: Magnificent Mess
Model 3: Creative Catastrophe
Model 4: Distinguished Dud
Model 5: Ketchupy Kerfuffle

The three friends cleaned up the mess. Then they shared peanut butter and honey sandwiches and talked about why the test failed.

After lunch, Ada and Iggy went home, and Rosie kept working. She looked at the contraption. A tube had exploded because a kink in the line blocked the ketchup. The pressure of the ketchup built up until—*BOOM!*

"Aha!" said Rosie.

She jotted down ideas to fix the problem. SnakeAway Model 6 would work better. She was sure of it. Well . . . she was almost sure. There was only one way to find out. She would make changes to the machine and test again.

Rosie was about to start when she heard a familiar whirring, purring, clanging, banging sound and looked out the window. It was Great-Great-Aunt Rose! Rosie stuck her pencil behind her ear, crammed her notebook into her pocket, and ran outside as Aunt Rose landed the heli-o-cheese-copter in the yard.

"Hey-hey!" called Aunt Rose. "How's my favorite engineer?"

Aunt Rose hopped out of the aircraft and twirled Rosie around in a giant hug.

"My new invention is a disaster!" said Rosie.

"Brilliant!" said Aunt Rose. "Tell me about it on the way!"

"Are we going somewhere?" asked Rosie.

"You bet we are," said Aunt Rose, "and there's no time to lose. This is an emergency!"

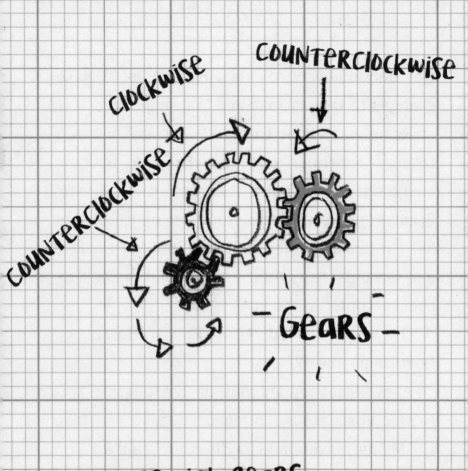

CLOCKWISE

COUNTERCLOCKWISE

COUNTERCLOCKWISE

COUNTERCLOCKWISE

– GEARS –

THINGS WITH GEARS

1. CARS
2. BIKES
3. CLOCKS
4. CHEESE-COPTER!

CHAPTER 3

Rosie put on her helmet, and Aunt Rose hit the switch. The cheese-copter sputtered and twitched. It jumped and bumped. It shot into the air . . . and off they flew!

They zoomed over the neighbor's garden.

"Woo-hoo! That's a doozy!" said Aunt Rose.

Indeed, Mrs. Lu's garden *was* a doozy. She was a master gardener, and it showed.

Each year, she planted flowers and grasses to create a giant scene in her yard. This year,

her plants looked like
a giant goose. Daisies,
asters, and marigolds painted
the picture. Tall, fluffy pampas stalks
completed the scene. They swayed in the breeze
and made the goose come to life.

Rosie looked down just as someone ran into
the garden shed wearing a long duster, a big hat,
dark glasses, and rubber gloves.

It was Mrs. Lu.

Rosie knew two things about Mrs. Lu:

1. She was mysterious. Rosie never saw her
   outside during the day without her disguise.
2. She did not like Rosie.

Mrs. Lu never said that. But then, she never
said anything to Rosie. They were neighbors, but
Mrs. Lu never even waved at Rosie. Once, Rosie
saw Mrs. Lu in the window and waved. Mrs. Lu
closed the curtains.

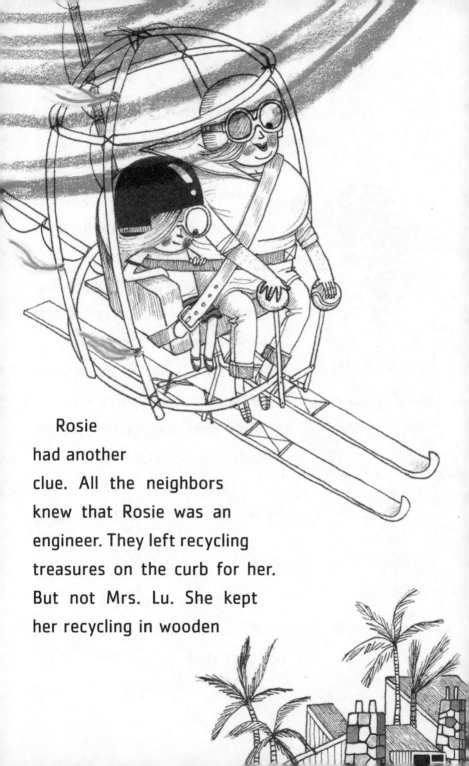

Rosie
had another
clue. All the neighbors
knew that Rosie was an
engineer. They left recycling
treasures on the curb for her.
But not Mrs. Lu. She kept
her recycling in wooden

crates on her porch instead of the curb. She didn't want Rosie getting into the crates. Luckily, the recyclers, Bee and Beau, sneaked the crates to Rosie's porch when she was at school.

Rosie was glad they did. The crates were full of gears and wire, tools, and broken motors. Mrs. Lu didn't like Rosie, but she sure had great recycling.

Aunt Rose steered the cheese-copter up, up, and away.

"Woo-hoo!" yelled Aunt Rose. "I do love a fancy garden!"

Rosie looked back at Mrs. Lu's garden shed just as a pair of gloved hands snapped the curtains shut.

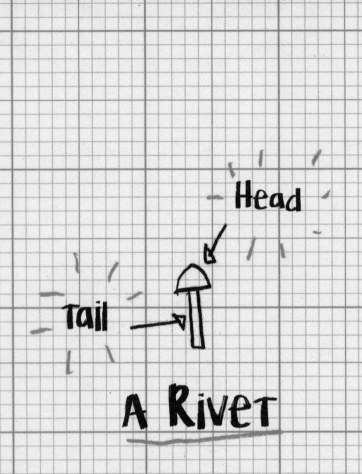

Head

Tail

A Rivet

CHAPTER 4

The cheese-copter flew past the school and Iggy Peck Bridge to the edge of town. Aunt Rose pointed at an old, white house with a wide porch.

"That's where we're going!" she said.

They landed with a *THUMP* and climbed out of the cheese-copter. The house needed a new coat of paint, and the yard was wild compared to Mrs. Lu's.

"We're here!" said Aunt Rose.

"Where is here?" asked Rosie.

"I have a better question. 'WHO is here?'" asked Aunt Rose.

Just then, the screen door flew open and a tall woman stepped onto the porch. She wore a red-and-white polka-dot headscarf. It was just like the one that Aunt Rose had given Rosie.

"About time you got here!" said the woman. "Boss is getting antsy."

"What else is new?" asked Aunt Rose.

They went into the house. The living room was faded but cozy. A set of old photos rested on a pump organ in one corner. They were black-and-white pictures of women working on enormous airplanes. A familiar face caught Rosie's eye. It was Aunt Rose. And she was young.

"Those are the Blue River Riveters," said Aunt Rose. "The smartest, sassiest, toughest bunch of airplane builders you ever saw."

"And the best dancers!" said the tall woman.

"And musicians!" yelled a woman's voice from the kitchen.

"Stop yakking and get that girl in here!" shouted another voice.

Aunt Rose nudged Rosie toward the kitchen.

"Don't keep Boss waiting!" she said.

They stepped into a large kitchen where five elderly women with coffee mugs sat around a well-worn wooden table.

As Rosie stepped into the room, they all cheered: "ROSIE!"

Suddenly, Rosie felt embarrassed and overwhelmed. Her cheeks got hot and she ducked behind Aunt Rose. Rosie didn't like being the center of attention.

"It's okay, kiddo," said Aunt Rose. "They don't bite. Except for Lettie. But she's just trying out her new false teeth!"

Aunt Rose slapped her knee and laughed out loud. "Oh, that's a good one!"

Aunt Rose laughed till she wheezed and her eyes filled with tears. Rosie relaxed and smiled.

The joke was not very funny, but Aunt Rose's laughter was contagious. Soon, all the women were laughing. Like Aunt Rose, they were loud and full of joy. They were raucous. And Rosie Revere decided that she liked them very much.

The woman in the wheelchair cleared her throat, and the others immediately got quiet. Every eye turned toward Rosie, and a twisty feeling creeped into her stomach.

"Well?" asked the woman. "What are you going to do?"

Rosie looked around nervously.

"About what?" she asked.

"What are you going to do about the emergency?" asked the woman. "After all, that's why you're here."

Things to do Today

go to ~~arkeology~~ archaeology shop
with Ada and Iggy

CHAPTER 5

"Give her a minute," said the tall woman, winking at Rosie. "She doesn't even know who we are!"

She shook Rosie's hand.

"I'm Lettie McCallister!" she said. "And these are my sisters, Heddie and Betty. We are musicians."

Two women in red waved at Rosie.

The woman sitting next to Betty smiled. "Rosie and I are old friends," she said.

Bernice was Ada's great-aunt. She owned the archaeology shop on the town square. It was called Can You Dig It? The shop was full of ancient things from around the world.

"Rosie and Ada and their friend, Iggy, come visit me all the time. These kids are so full of ideas and questions that I gave them a nickname! I call them the Questioneers!"

"Oh, I like that!" said Aunt Rose.

The other women nodded.

Rosie liked it, too. Visiting the Can You Dig It? shop was always an adventure, and Bernice was full of ideas and questions. She was one of Rosie's favorite people.

"I have new treasures in the shop," Bernice said. "Bring Ada and Iggy to see them!"

"I will!" said Rosie.

"We have another singer in the group!" said Betty McCallister. "This is Marian, and she sings opera. Wait until you hear her!"

"A pleasure to meet you," said Marian.

She was formal and elegant, with silvery hair, a strand of pearls, and a twinkle in her eyes. She smiled at Rosie.

Rosie smiled back.

"And lastly," said the woman in the wheelchair. "I'm Eleanor. But you can call me Boss. Everybody does."

"Because you're bossy!" joked Lettie.

"I speak plain and I get things done," said Boss. "If that makes me bossy, then good! I am too busy getting things done to care!"

The Riveters cheered.

Boss smiled.

"We are the Blue River Riveters," she said. "We worked together at the B-29 factory during World War II. We built more airplanes than you could imagine. We made a difference back when it was needed the most. And we still do our part!"

"You're the women in the photo!" said Rosie. "But where are the others?"

"It was a long time ago, dear," said Marian. "We've lost many friends."

Her voice grew quiet.

"So many," said Lettie.

The Riveters raised their coffee mugs with one hand and slapped the table with the other.

"To friends!" they cheered.

BlUE RiVER creek

Art-a-go-go!

CHAPTER 6

After a moment, Boss slapped the table again. "The McCallister sisters let us use their house as our own home," she said.

"It's your home, too!" said Betty. "We've all known one another so long, we're family!"

Rosie liked that. She lived with all her aunts and uncles and knew that families came in all shapes and sizes.

"We always help one another in an emergency," said Lettie.

"And sometimes, we get together and just dance," said Aunt Rose.

"Yeah, we do!" said Heddie.

She tapped out a beat on her coffee mug. Lettie and Betty broke into a zippy song about doing the boogie-woogie and jumping the jive. The Riveters swayed and clapped along.

WHACK!

Boss slapped the table hard and the room went silent.

"Riveters! Have you forgotten our emergency?" said Boss. "We have to help June!"

"Sorry, Boss," said Heddie, not looking very sorry at all. "I got carried away there."

"Then get carried right back here!" said Boss. "You can start by telling Rosie what's going on."

Heddie and the Riveters told Rosie about June, the artist of the bunch. During the war, June painted the pictures on the noses of the airplanes. Each year since, June painted in the art contest at the Blue River Creek Festival. It was the most important event of the year for her.

A few months ago, June wrecked her motor-scooter and broke both her wrists. Her wrists were very weak, so she still wore casts.

"How can she paint with casts?" asked Rosie.

Boss stared hard at Rosie.

"That," she said, "is up to you."

Aunt Rose handed Rosie a flyer.

ART-A-GO-GO

**SATURDAY 9:30 A.M. MEET AT TOWN LIBRARY
TO RECEIVE THE THEME OF THE CONTEST.
2:00 P.M. JUDGING BEGINS.
ARTISTS MUST PAINT BY THEMSELVES.
SUPPORT TEAMS CAN SET UP, CLEAN UP, AND CHEER!
NO ELECTRICITY CAN BE USED.**

"June is having a hard time," said Aunt Rose. "So we are going to surprise her. It's top secret! We will take turns keeping June busy. Then we'll sneak her to the contest without her suspecting anything at all."

"We'll all do our part," said Boss.

Boss's smile faded and she looked squarely at Rosie.

"What about you, Rosie," she asked. "Will you do *your* part?"

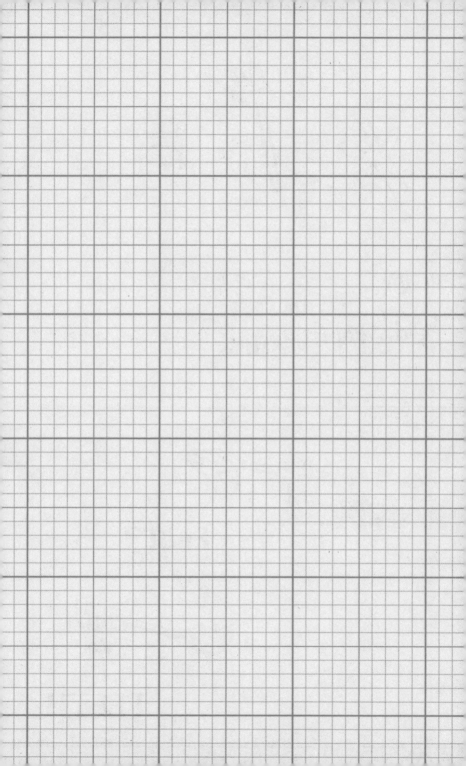

= = =

OTHER ways to hold a PAINTbRUSH?

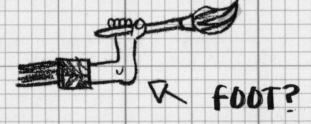

FOOT?

TEETH?

CHAPTER 7

Rosie nodded.

She read the flyer again.

"The artists have to create the art by themselves," she said. "If I can't help June paint, what can I do?"

"You're an engineer!" said Lettie. "Invent something!"

"June's art comes from her heart," said Marian. "She just needs the tools to help her hands."

"But the contest is only two days from now!" said Rosie.

"Better get thinking!" said Boss.

She spoke too late. Rosie was already thinking. She had so many questions: How could she build a painting machine? How would it load paint? What kind of paint? How many colors? How would June control the brushes without using her hands? How . . .

Rosie flipped open her notebook. She jotted furiously to catch the ideas exploding in her mind. As she did, the sounds of the chattering Riveters faded away, and Rosie was pulled into her own world of engineering.

Rosie loved engineering. It made her happier than just about anything. And her very favorite part was right at the start.

She jotted down her ideas. Then she noticed that everything was silent. She stopped scribbling and looked up. Seven smiling Riveters stood watching her.

They raised their coffee mugs in a silent toast to Rosie.

"I told you she was up to it," said Aunt Rose.

"Indeed she is," said Boss. "Indeed she is."

Rosie felt her cheeks turn red, but this time, she did not duck behind Aunt Rose.

Rosie Revere looked at the smiling Riveters and smiled back.

PAINTBRUSH

JUMP

CHAPTER 8

Two days!

Rosie had less than two days to invent a contraption to help June. The task was almost too great to imagine. But that didn't stop Rosie from trying.

When she got home, she went straight to her attic room. She felt a storm approaching. A brainstorm!

Rosie loved brainstorming. Anything was possible. Even crazy, weird ideas. Sometimes,

Rosie's weirdest ideas made her think in a new way or solved tiny bits of a big problem. She wrote all her ideas in her notebook.

What if she made a cat-powered painting pump?

It would need a lot of cats. And milk. It would probably flop. After all, cats always run off or sit around like lazy lumps. How could she get a lazy, lumpy cat to power a painting machine?

Rosie sketched her idea anyhow.

What if she made a Paint Blobber that used a small catapult to chuck balls of paint at the canvas?

What if she combined the two ideas and made a *Cat-a-pult*? Would the cats like it? What would that look like? Rosie sketched it out.

Rosie had lots of questions. What she did NOT have was time. If she spent too long brainstorming, she would run out of time to make and test the invention. Testing was tricky.

She remembered the ketchup explosion and the big mess it—

Wait a minute! thought Rosie.

A new question popped into Rosie's mind. Could the SnakeAway help? What if it pumped paint instead of ketchup?

Rosie decided that this was a good place to start. The SnakeAway used a small pump from the garden pond. It ran on batteries and was too small, but Rosie could use it to figure out the brushing mechanism. After that, she could figure out how to pump the paint without a battery. Step by step, she would solve this problem.

Rosie smiled.

It was time for the next stage of the process: design!

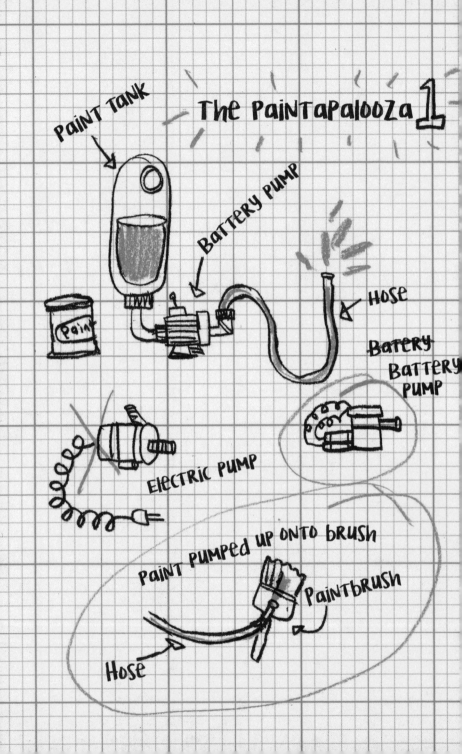

PAINT TANK

THE PAINTAPALOOZA 1

BATTERY PUMP

HOSE

Batery
BATTERY
PUMP

ELECTRIC PUMP

PAINT PUMPED UP ONTO bRUSh

Paintbrush

Hose

CHAPTER 9

Brainstorming was Rosie's favorite part of engineering. But so was design. And research! And making prototypes! And testing!

In truth, Rosie could not pick a favorite part of engineering. That was like picking a favorite cheese. How could a person pick just one? And why would they want to?

Rosie tied up her headscarf. She dumped a pile of engineering treasure on the table next to the broken SnakeAway Model 5 and got working.

After three hours, she completed the first model of her new invention: the Paintapalooza 1.

It was funky. It was weird.

But, thought Rosie, *it just might work.*

She set her easel in the yard and put the Paintapalooza on the ground next to it. She grabbed her goggles and called to Gizmo, who was watching from a tree branch.

"Stay up there!" Rosie yelled.

Gizmo looped the loop, landed on her branch, and chirped.

"Me, too!" said Rosie.

Rosie put on her goggles and filled the tank with red paint. Then she kicked the switch with her toe. A line of red paint snaked through the clear tube and flowed onto the paintbrush. It was working!

Rosie stepped up to the easel, reached out, and—

SNAP!

PFSSSSSSSSSSSSSSSSSSSSSSSSSSSSSSSSSTTTTT!

The hose broke free! It slashed through the air like an angry cobra, spitting red paint everywhere. Back and forth. Back and forth. Up and around.

Rosie swiped at the hose but could not grab it. Paint sprayed over her dress and onto her face and safety goggles. She couldn't see where she was going!

Rosie took a step and—

CRACK!

Her foot broke the leg of the easel.

"Whoa!"

Rosie tripped, flipped, and landed on her back with a *THUD!* The easel teetered then tottered then fell on top of her. *CRASH!*

She lay on the ground beneath the easel and sighed.

Rosie knew that failing was part of engineering,

but she didn't like it. The Raucous Riveters were counting on her, and she could not let them down.

Rosie shook her head.

"STOP AND THINK!" she said.

Rosie thought about what had gone wrong with the test: The loose tube was easy to fix. Rosie felt a little better. She asked another question: What had gone *right* with the test? The pump got the paint through the tube. That was a big deal. She was on the right track.

Rosie smiled as the sun hit her painted goggles and they glowed like stained-glass windows.

At least no one saw me, thought Rosie. *That was good . . .*

And that's when Rosie heard footsteps.

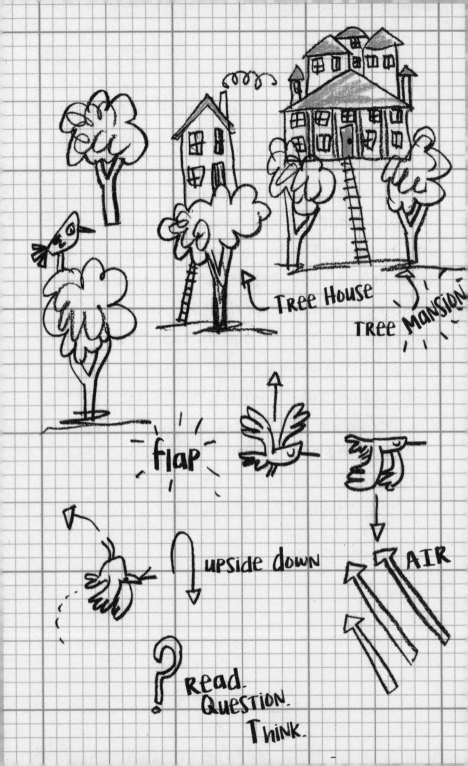

Tree House

Tree MANSION

flap

upside down

AIR

read.
Question.
Think.

CHAPTER 10

Rosie!" said Ada.

Rosie breathed a sigh of relief. It was Ada and Iggy.

"What are you doing?" asked Iggy.

"I'm just thinking," said Rosie.

"We'll help!" said Ada.

Ada and Iggy moved the easel and plopped onto the ground next to Rosie. They looked up at the tree and smiled. Just like Rosie, they loved thinking about things. They were full of questions. Bernice was right. They really were Questioneers.

"That tree needs a tree house," said Iggy, and he thought about how to make one.

"Why do birds live in trees?" asked Ada. "How do birds fly? Can they fly upside down?"

Ada thought about trees and birds and flying and so many other things.

It's nice to have friends, thought Rosie.

She was glad that her friends had come over. They understood her. They also understood what it was like to get caught up in a project. Ada Twist was a scientist and Iggy Peck was an architect. They always helped one another.

The three friends lay beneath the tree for a long time. Rosie told them about the Raucous Riveters and the Art-a-Go-Go contest. They had some good ideas. It helped Rosie to brainstorm with friends.

Rosie heard a rustle in the bushes. She turned around and looked toward Mrs. Lu's yard, but no one was there.

"Time to go back to the drawing board," said Rosie.

Ada looked at the broken easel.

"Time to get a new drawing board," she said.

"The broken one would make a great chalet for Ada's cat," said Iggy.

Iggy was right. Ada's cat would love a triangle-shaped Swiss house called a chalet. As Iggy and Ada carried away the easel, Gizmo flew down from the tree and rested on Rosie's shoulder.

"Ready for Paintapalooza 2?" asked Rosie.

Gizmo chirped.

"Yep. This is going to take a lot of paint," said Rosie. "We're gonna need a bigger bucket. And more plastic tubing."

Gizmo chirped again.

"You're right!" said Rosie. "We need more tape! Lots and lots of tape."

Things to get for the Paintapalooza

Painting gloves

A **Big** Bucket

Tape

Plastic Tubing

CHAPTER 11

By bedtime, Rosie had a basic model of the Paintapalooza 2. But she had so much more to do. She needed big painting gloves and a bigger pump June could use without electricity. But Rosie was too tired to keep working.

She went to bed but could not sleep. She was worried. What if she didn't finish in time? What if the contraption squirted the crowd with paint? What if somebody knocked it over? What if—

"STOP AND THINK!" Rosie said out loud.

Rosie had a great imagination. It made her a great engineer. But sometimes, her What-Ifs got carried away. When that happened, Rosie had to remind herself to stop and think differently. It was a trick that Aunt Rose taught her. It helped her stay on track. And it helped her feel better.

Rosie relaxed and breathed deeply. That was another trick to get calm that she knew. Moonlight spilled into her room and lit her bed with a grayish glow. At last, her eyelids grew heavy and Rosie drifted to—*CLIP! SNIP! SCRAPE!*

Rosie jumped out of bed and looked out the window. The noises stopped. She strained to see into the dark. Was that a figure in the shadows of Mrs. Lu's garden? Rosie rubbed her eyes and looked again. She saw only shadows.

The pampas grass glowed dimly in the moonlight and swayed in the cool night breeze. Suddenly, a chill passed over Rosie. She climbed back into bed and pulled the covers up to her chin.

Rosie shook away the image of the shadowy figure and thought about buckets and pumps and painting. Slowly her eyelids grew heavier and heavier. Then, at last, Rosie Revere slept.

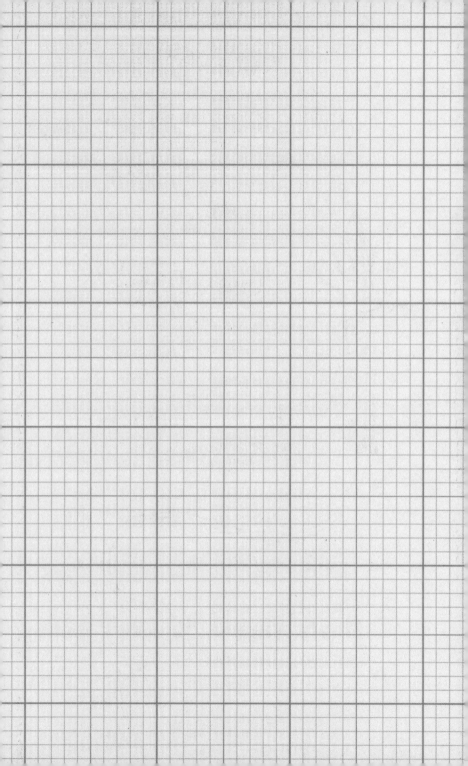

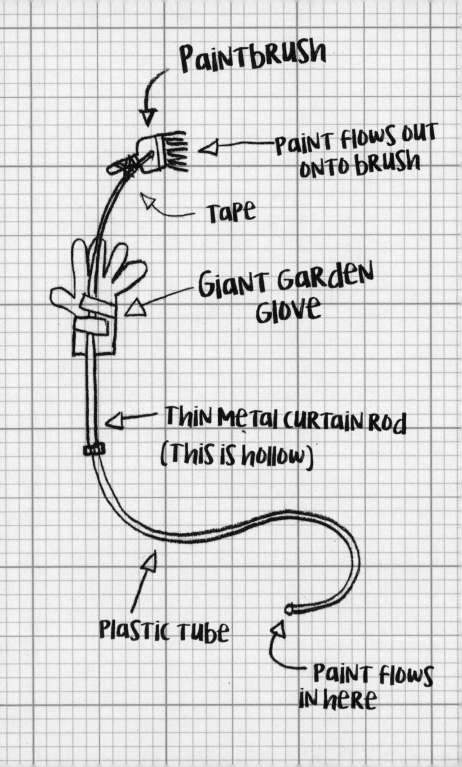

PAINTBRUSH

PAINT FLOWS OUT ONTO BRUSH

TAPE

GIANT GARDEN GLOVE

THIN METAL CURTAIN ROD (THIS IS hollow)

PLASTIC TUBE

PAINT FLOWS IN HERE

CHAPTER 12

Rosie woke early and hopped out of bed. The Blue River Creek Festival was one day away, and she still needed a working pump! Rosie went outside. Iggy and Ada were already in the yard, filling small jars with paint and water. They were doing an experiment to find the perfect mixture.

"If it's too thick, it won't flow through the tubes," said Ada. "If it's too thin, it will drip off the canvas."

Rosie went to the patio to get a small table for the Paintapalooza. A big blue bucket sat on the table. It was filled with plastic tubing and waterproof tape.

"Thanks for getting this stuff!" Rosie yelled to her friends.

They were too busy to notice.

As Rosie worked on the pump, Ada and Iggy experimented, and Gizmo chirped from the tree.

Rosie attached thin metal curtain rods from the thrift shop to a giant pair of garden gloves. Then she added the brushes. They were long enough to reach the edges of the canvas. Next she used strings and springs and other things to make a paint-switcher, so June could change colors while she worked.

Ada and Iggy made progress. After two hours, the team had the perfect paint formula and a working set of brush gloves. They had everything EXCEPT a pump.

Rosie was still worried. If she didn't come up with a pump, the Paintapalooza would flop. But much worse, June's surprise would be ruined. The Art-a-Go-Go would be a no-go!

Rosie and her friends could not let that happen.

They worked and worked. They tried this, that, and the other thing. As the hours ticked away, so did Rosie's patience.

"Why don't we take a break," asked Ada. "A time-out helps me think better."

"We need more paint," said Iggy. "Let's go get some."

"You and Ada go," said Rosie. "I'll keep working."

Ada and Iggy grabbed Rosie's wagon and headed to the Happy Sapling Art Store.

WE CAN DO IT!

Rosie looked around the yard. It was a mess. The grass was filled with puddles of paint. She turned around and stepped right into a big bucket of blue paint.

SPLOOP!

Blue paint glopped all over her red shoe. Frustration boiled up inside Rosie. She wanted to throw the bucket and the Paintapalooza into the trash can.

"UGH!" shouted Rosie. She kicked her foot to shake off the paint.

ZOOOOOOP!

Rosie's shoe flew off! It soared through the air and smacked into the tree right next to Gizmo.

Gizmo chirped angrily and flew off.

"I'm sorry, Gizmo!" yelled Rosie.

Rosie chased the bird, leaving a trail of blue footprints as she went. But Gizmo was too fast. Halfway around the block, Rosie gave up.

She was frustrated and frazzled. She couldn't

think straight. But that was exactly what she needed to do.

"STOP AND THINK!" Rosie said.

Rosie plopped down beneath a tree. She took a deep breath and tried to calm down. It helped. A little.

Ada was right, thought Rosie. *I need a break.*

Rosie got up and walked down the sidewalk. As she walked, her anger faded, like her blue footprints on the concrete. With each step, the prints were lighter and so was her mood.

She hoped Gizmo would be waiting for her at home. And that's right where Rosie found her. But she was not alone.

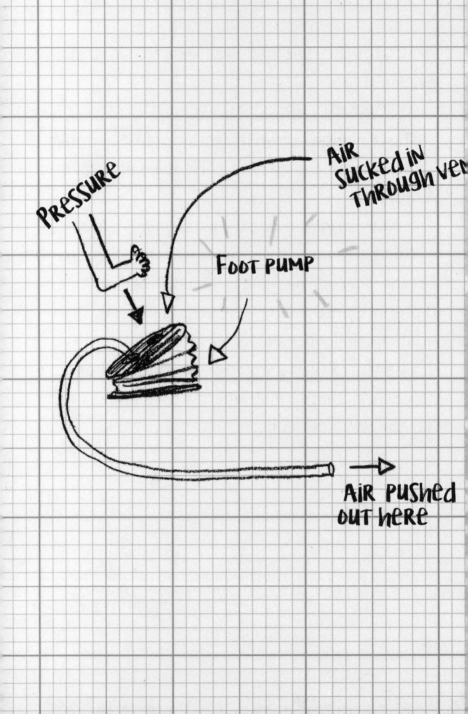

Pressure

Air sucked in through ven

Foot pump

Air pushed out here

CHAPTER 13

As Rosie turned the corner, a strange droning sound filled the air. Then, someone yelled, "One! Two! A one-two-three-four!"

And then there was music! It was the McCallisters on the bed of a big, old army truck, right in front of Rosie's house! The droning sound was Heddie on the bagpipes. Betty played the pump organ, and Lettie played the accordion.

The Raucous Riveters danced in the street in front of the truck. They twirled and swirled and jumped to the jive. Rosie's family and neighbors poured out of their houses and joined in the fun.

The Riveters all sang:

We can rivet, weld, and hammer.
And we do it just fine.
Building ships and planes and trucks
  on the assembly line.
We can do it! We can do it!
Each and every one.
And we'll do our part. Right from the start.
Until the job's done.

Gizmo flew to Rosie, looped the loop, and zoomed back to the organ, where Aunt Rose's bird, Gadget, tweeted along with the music.

"Hey-hey!" said Aunt Rose when Rosie reached the crowd. "We thought you could use a dance party."

She tapped her cane along with the music.

"How is it going?" she asked.

"I'm stuck," said Rosie.

"Dance it off!" said Aunt Rose. "Show us some moves!"

The music was catchy, and before she knew it, Rosie was tapping her foot. Then she was dancing. It was a right raucous time, and for a few minutes, Rosie forgot all about the pump.

Ada and Iggy came back with a wagon full of paint cans. They parked the wagon and jumped into the dance. Each of the kids had their own dance moves. Before long, the Riveters were doing the Skyscraper with Iggy. Ada taught them the Molecule. Rosie had everyone spinning around, doing the Gyroscope.

Rosie had never heard a trio like the McCallister sisters. She especially loved the bagpipes. Heddie blew into a mouthpiece to fill the leather bag. Then she squeezed the bag with her arm. Each squeeze pushed air through the musical pipe.

Her fingers danced over the holes and played a jumping, jazzy tune.

Lettie stretched the accordion to suck in air. Then she squeezed it and pressed keys to play notes. Betty stepped on the foot pedal of the organ while her hands flew up and down the keyboard. Each instrument pumped in air and held it until a note was played. How did that work? Why didn't the air whoosh out of the instruments as soon as the pumping stopped? Something blocked the air from flowing backward.

These questions swirled like music in Rosie's mind. She didn't notice that she had stopped dancing. She was thinking. AND she was onto an answer.

Then, suddenly, Rosie Revere knew EXACTLY what she needed! A valve!

For the next hour, the McCallisters played and sang, and Ada, Iggy, and the crowd danced to the swinging music. No one even noticed that Rosie was gone.

The music drifted to Rosie's backyard, where she worked furiously. She did not notice the faint snipping and clipping noises beyond the hedge keeping time with the music.

Rosie was too busy smiling at the finished Paintapalooza 3 to notice anything at all.

HOW VALVES WORK

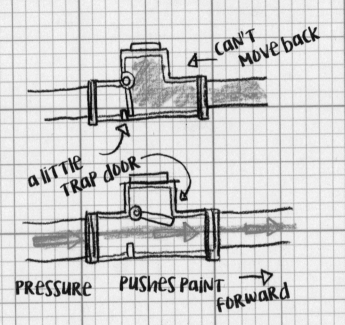

CAN'T MOVE BACK

a little TRAP DOOR

PRESSURE PUSHES PAINT FORWARD

CHAPTER 14

At nine o'clock the next morning, Ada and Iggy showed up at Rosie's. They loaded the wagon and covered it with a sheet. Then they headed to the Blue River Creek library.

A dozen canvases surrounded the parking lot. Rosie found Aunt Rose, Boss, Marian, and the McCallister sisters in the corner.

"Rosie!" they cheered. "Ada! Iggy!"

Just then, Bernice arrived with a woman in a big floppy hat with casts on her wrists. It had to be June.

"Okay," said Bernice. "We're here!"

She took off June's hat.

"Surprise!" yelled the Riveters.

June looked from face to face in shock.

"What? Why . . ." she started. "What's going—"

"It's Art-a-Go-Go time!" said Boss.

June was shocked.

"But I have casts," she said, raising her arms.

"The Riveters wanted to surprise you,"
said Rosie. "So . . .

ta-daaaa!"

Ada and Iggy pulled the sheet off the wagon. June looked baffled.

"It's the Paintapalooza 9!" said Rosie proudly. "It took a few tries, but I think we finally did it."

June looked even more baffled, but she tried to hide it.

"Well, thank you, dear," she said. "I always wanted one."

"What is it?" She whispered to Aunt Rose.

Boss shook her head.

"Oh, you goofball!" she said. "The kids created an invention so you can paint with your arms instead of your hands!"

Tears welled up in June's eyes.

"I . . ." she said softly, then stopped.

A tear rolled down her cheek.

"Oh, you Riveters," she said. "You are the best."

"And you three!" she said to Rosie and her friends. "I don't even know what . . ."

Her voice trailed off as she choked back tears.

Boss cleared her throat loudly.

"Enough of that mushy stuff!" she said with a sniffle. "You know I'm allergic to crying. It makes my eyes water!"

June and the Riveters burst into laughter.

Then, suddenly—*SQUEEEEEEEEEAK!*

A sharp squeal blasted over the loudspeaker.

"Attention!" said a librarian. "Are you ready for Art-a-Go-Go?"

"Go! Go!" the crowd cheered.

June dried her eyes with her sleeve and smiled.

"Yes, I am!" she said.

She smiled at Rosie, Ada, and Iggy.

"Thanks to you," she said.

The librarian announced, "This year's theme for the Art-a-Go-Go competition is 'Home'!"

He blew the whistle again and it was time to go-go!

I 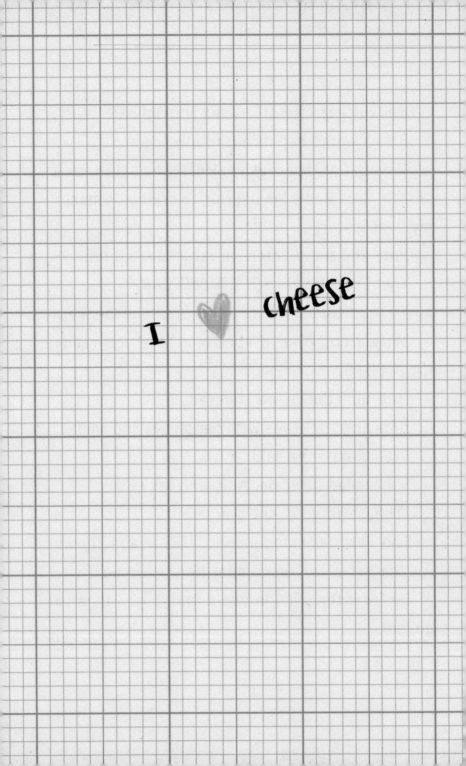 cheese

CHAPTER 15

Rosie set up the Paintapalooza and helped June into the gloves.

"Are they okay?" asked Rosie.

"They're weird but okay," said June. "I am ready to paint!"

June stood in front of the blank canvas.

"This is the exciting part," she said. "I love brainstorming!"

"Me, too!" said Rosie.

June stepped onto the foot pump. Rosie,

Ada, and Iggy watched nervously. The Raucous Riveters held their breath.

Pump. Pump. Pump.

Nothing happened.

Pump. Pump. Pump.

Nothing.

Pump. Pump.

Rosie's heart sank.

Pump.

Suddenly, paint snaked through the tubes. The Paintapalooza worked!

The Riveters cheered and clapped. June gently tapped the red button with her shoe. A glob of red paint squirted onto the red brush. She made a smooth, even stroke on the canvas.

June pushed the blue button and a glob of blue paint squeezed onto the blue brush. She dabbed it onto the canvas and began to paint. The Paintapalooza was working beautifully and June was smiling.

Then she wasn't.

"The only true failure
can come if you quit."
—Aunt Rose

CHAPTER 16

"O uch," she cried.

"What happened?" asked Rosie.

"My arm is sore," said June.

She reached up again.

"Ow," she said. "Maybe I should rest."

She tried again a few minutes later.

"Oh dear," she said. "My arms are too weak."

Rosie's heart sank.

June smiled kindly at her.

"Rosie," she said. "I want you to finish the painting."

Rosie shook her head. If anyone but June painted, she would be out of the contest.

"Rosie," said June softly. "I *want* you to paint. Truly."

Rosie looked at June's face and knew that she meant it.

"I'm sorry it was too heavy," said Rosie.

"The Paintapalooza was perfect," said June. "I will use it to paint my kitchen when my arms are stronger!"

She laughed out loud, and Rosie smiled.

Rosie tightened her headscarf. She picked up the left glove and—*BOOM!*

An idea hit Rosie's brain like thunder. And what an idea! She took off the paint glove and handed it to Aunt Rose.

"Don't let anyone touch that canvas!" said Rosie. "I'll be back!"

And with that, Rosie ran down the street and was gone.

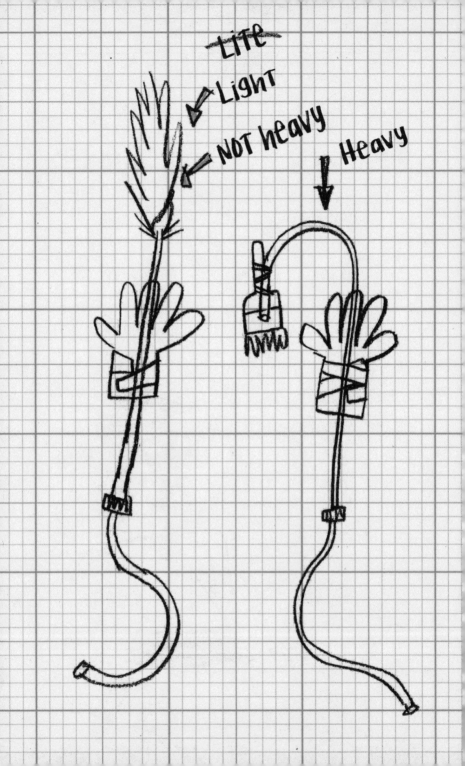

CHAPTER 17

Rosie ran down Milk Lane, past Wells Drive, to Rains Street, with Gizmo zooming behind her. She stopped to catch her breath, then went to Mrs. Lu's house.

Rosie climbed the porch steps. Then, she took another deep breath. She was nervous. She knew how to help June, but she needed Mrs. Lu's help. What if Mrs. Lu said no?

Rosie wished she was back at the library with Ada, Iggy, and the Riveters. She almost turned around to leave, but then she thought about June. She had promised to do her part.

Rosie had to be brave.

"You can do it," Rosie said to herself.

Gizmo perched on Rosie's shoulder and chirped.

"I know," said Rosie, and she rang the doorbell.

Rosie waited. No answer. She rang again. No answer.

She knocked loudly.

"Hello?" she yelled. "Mrs. Lu?"

Silence.

Rosie's heart sank. She turned away from the door.

Suddenly, Gizmo flew in front of her. She flapped her wings furiously and looped the loop, blocking Rosie's way.

"What's wrong?" asked Rosie.

"CHIRP! CHIRP! CHIRP!"

"Stop it, Gizmo!" said Rosie.

"CHIRP! CHIRP!"

CRACKLE.

Rosie heard a strange noise behind her.

CRACKLE.

"Hello?" said a faint, scratchy voice.

It came from a box in the corner of the porch.
Rosie looked into the box.

"Hello?" she said.

A purple metal goose looked
back at her with googly eyes.

CRACKLE.

"Stay there!" said a
scratchy voice.

It came from the
metal goose. Rosie
leaned closer.

Just then, the door opened. Mrs. Lu stepped outside. She held a strange walkie-talkie handset.

"Sorry," she said. "My Goosey-Talkie is not working!"

She pushed a button on the back of the goose. She clicked a button on her handset. The goose's beak snapped open.

CRACKLE.

"Hello? Hello?" Mrs. Lu spoke into her handset and her voice came out of the goose's mouth. "That's more like it!"

Then she tossed the handset into the box and smiled.

"Hello, Rosie!" she said. "Glad to see you!"

Rosie was shocked. Mrs. Lu was so friendly. Rosie thought about how Mrs. Lu had shut the curtains on her and how she sneaked like a shadow in the garden.

Rosie looked at her neighbor and felt more nervous than ever.

"I . . ." she said. "I . . ."

"Yes?" asked Mrs. Lu.

Rosie took another deep breath and remembered why she was there.

"I need your help," she said.

Mrs. Lu smiled.

"I thought you'd never ask!"

Fluffy end

Pampas gras

Stalk

Hollow and Light

Paint can flow up the stalk and onto the fluffy end.

CHAPTER 18

*B*EEP! BEEP!

The old army jeep zoomed around the corner and toward the library.

A load of pampas stalks bounced around in the back of the jeep.

BEEP! BEEP!

The jeep screeched to a halt a few feet from June's canvas.

"Would you look at that?!" cried Boss. "It's Agnes Lu!"

"And Rosie!" said Ada.

She and Iggy ran to the jeep.

"Rosie!" they said. "What's going on?"

Rosie flipped open the glove box and Gizmo hopped out. She chirped happily and flew to the top of the canvas.

"June needed lighter brushes," Rosie said. "So I asked Mrs. Lu if we could use one of the pampas stalks from her garden. She cut them ALL down!"

Mrs. Lu and Rosie jumped out of the jeep and grabbed a bunch of plumes from the back.

"Agnes Lu!" said Aunt Rose. "What have you done to your beautiful garden?"

"Doesn't matter," said Mrs. Lu. "When a Riveter needs something, I do my part! June needs these more than I do."

She pulled a pair of shears from the pocket of her duster and trimmed one of the stalks.

"They're lighter than those curtain rods," said

Mrs. Lu, "Though I would have tried curtain rods, too. It was a good design."

Rosie looked confused.

"You design things?" she asked.

Mrs. Lu laughed.

"Well, of course I do!" she said. "I'm an engineer, too. And we engineers have to help each other. That's why I left the bucket of tubes and tape for you!"

Rosie thought those had come from Ada and Iggy or the recyclers, Bee and Beau. She had so many questions but no time to ask them. Aunt Rose and the Riveters crowded in to give Mrs. Lu hugs. They all knew her!

"Your poor garden!" said June. "What were you thinking?"

Mrs. Lu raised her hand.

"Not another word!" she said. "It's time to paint!"

Mrs. Lu handed Rosie a stalk, and Rosie got busy.

Within moments, June was painting again. She swished the brushes this way and that. It was beautiful.

Then—*SNAP!*—the red stem broke.

"Uh-oh!" said Rosie.

"That's why we brought extras!" said Mrs. Lu.

THINGS THAT
have RIVETS

① SHIPS
② AIRPLANES
③ JEEPS
④ JEANS

solid Rivet

Round
RIVETS

Round

COUNTERSUNK

flat

Pan

RIVETS

CHAPTER 19

Rosie swapped in a new stalk, and June kept painting. After a few minutes, the blue stem snapped, but Rosie was ready with a replacement. As other stems broke, Rosie swapped them, too.

Meanwhile, Rosie, Ada, and Iggy learned more about the mysterious Mrs. Lu. Boss explained that Mrs. Lu was a Riveter in the jeep factory on the other side of the river from the airplane factory.

"I made this very jeep!" said Mrs. Lu. "I learned a lot about machines during the war. It made me want to invent some, so I did! Haven't stopped since."

Rosie was amazed. All this time, she had lived next door to another engineer and didn't know it!

Mrs. Lu seemed to read her mind.

"You didn't know because I rarely get out of the house except at night," she said. "I have a skin condition that makes me allergic to sunlight. It's why I wear this crazy garb. Can't let the sun hit me."

"Is that why you keep your curtains shut?" asked Rosie.

"Yes," said Mrs. Lu. "But your Aunt Rose lets me know when you've got a project, and I donate what I can to help. I'm glad you like the crates I leave at your house."

"You do that?" asked Rosie.

"Of course!" said Mrs. Lu. "Did you think it was the Tooth Fairy?"

"More like the Tool Fairy!" said Aunt Rose. "Oh, that's a good one!"

Aunt Rose slapped her knee and laughed out loud. She laughed until she wheezed and her eyes filled with tears. Soon, the whole group was laughing. No one laughed harder than Mrs. Lu.

Rosie realized that she had been very wrong about Mrs. Lu. She thought Mrs. Lu was mean and mysterious and did not like her. She should have given Mrs. Lu a chance.

Mrs. Lu smiled at Rosie.

"You know, Rosie," she said. "I could use your help with a doohickey I made to scrub the dishes. It's simply smashing."

"It sounds amazing," said Rosie.

"No!" said Mrs. Lu. "It is simply smashing all my plates! And now I'm almost out of bowls!"

She laughed again. Rosie laughed, too.

"I'd love to help," said Rosie.

"It's good to have an engineer for a neighbor," said Mrs. Lu.

Rosie smiled back. It is indeed.

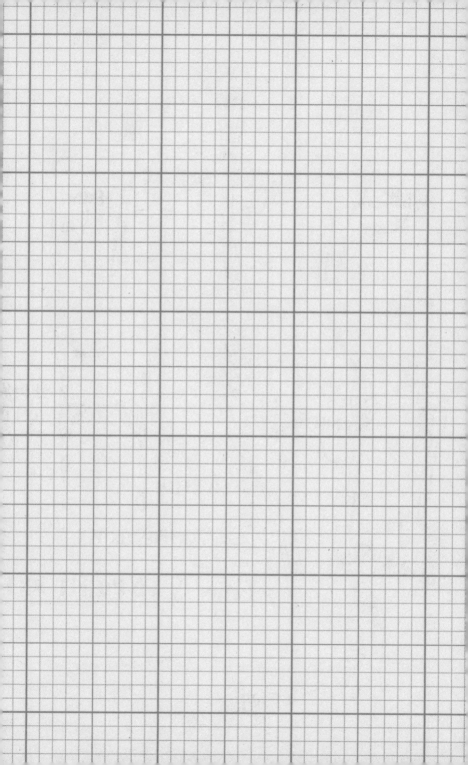

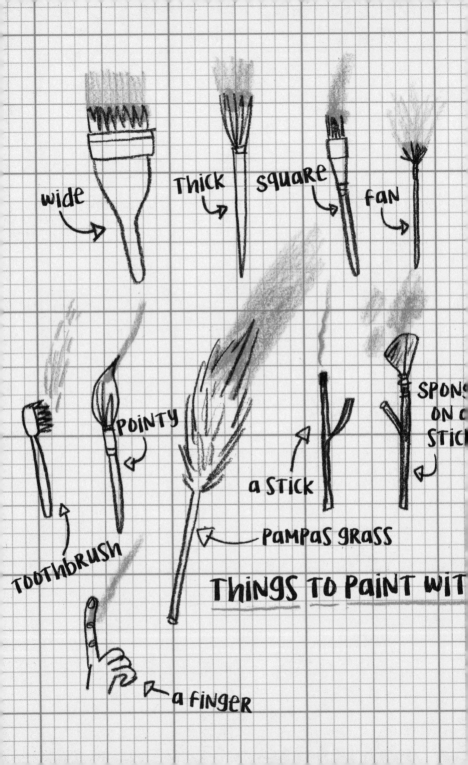

wide

Thick

square

fan

POINTY

toothbrush

a STICK

PAMPAS GRASS

SPONG
ON
STIC

THINGS TO PAINT WIT

a finger

CHAPTER 20

The parking lot was full of artists and their families. The McCallister sisters and Marian borrowed the librarian's microphone and sang to the crowd while the artists painted. There was dancing and laughing. Everyone was having a great time.

Especially June.

She grinned as she swished her arms left and right and up and down over the canvas. The Paintapalooza was working like a charm.

Then, June reached up and—

"Ouch! Ouch!" she cried. "Double ouch!"

Her face wrinkled up in pain.

"What's wrong?" asked Iggy.

"I have to stop," said June. "My wrists hurt."

Rosie helped June take off the gloves. She looked at them sadly The Paintapalooza had worked, but it still didn't help June. The whole adventure was a flop.

Rosie frowned.

But June grinned. Then, June chuckled. Then, she laughed out loud.

Rosie was shocked.

"What's funny?" she asked. "You have to quit painting!"

"Who's quitting?" asked June. "Maybe I can't paint, but you all can!"

"But if we paint, then you can't win the contest," Rosie said.

"Oh, Rosie," June said softly. "Don't you see? I've already won. This is the most fun I've had in years!"

Rosie smiled. Iggy and Ada cheered. The Riveters cheered, too.

"C'mon everyone, let's finish the painting together!" June cried.

They all grabbed paintbrushes and pampas stalks and got painting. When they were done, they stood back and admired the canvas.

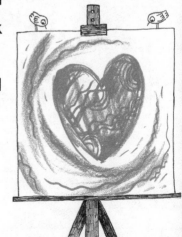

"Home sweet home," said June. "It's perfect."

FAVORITE VALVES

1. Ball valve
2. Butterfly valve
3. Clapper valve
4. Choke valve
5. Gate valve
6. Needle valve
7. Poppet valve

CHAPTER 21

Suddenly, Boss slapped her hand on the arm of her wheelchair, and the Riveters grew silent. Boss motioned for Mrs. Lu and the Riveters to gather around her.

Rosie, Ada, and Iggy stood by the canvas.

"What's going on?" Ada asked.

"I don't know," said Rosie. "But I think it's serious."

The Riveters huddled. They whispered to one another and took turns glancing at the kids.

Finally, the huddle broke apart and Boss wheeled to the canvas. The Riveters stood silently behind her.

Boss spoke in a clear, strong voice.

"I speak for us all. Including our dear Agnes," she said.

Agnes Lu smiled and put a hand on Boss's shoulder.

"We are the Riveters," said Boss. "We do our part. We always have and we always will. It's who we are."

The women smiled proudly.

"That means taking care of one another," said Boss. "That's what makes us a family."

June stepped forward.

"Rosie, Ada, and Iggy," she said. "You did something important when you made that contraption. You helped someone you didn't even know. You did your part."

"You did indeed," said Boss. "And today, we declare that you are honorary Riveters!"

Betty, Lettie, and Heddy McCallister stepped forward.

"We further declare that our home is now officially your home, too," they said. "That includes all the singing and dancing you can handle!"

"We can handle a lot of dancing!" said Iggy.

"Zowie!" said Ada.

"Thank you," said Rosie.

"Three cheers for Iggy and Ada! Three cheers for Rosie Revere! Three cheers for the Questioneers!"

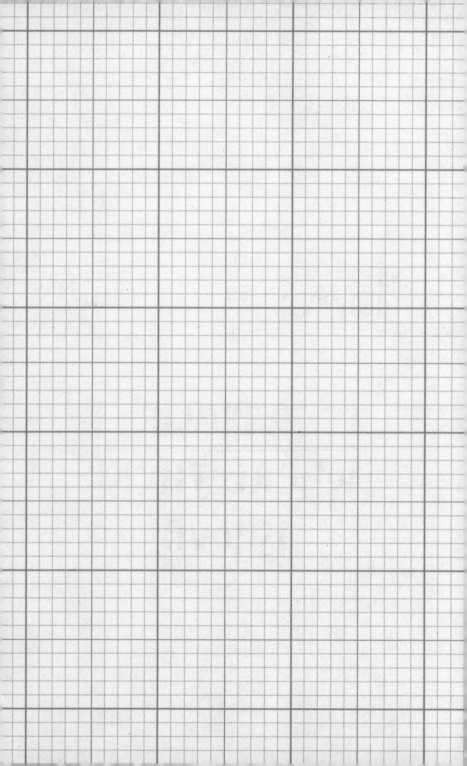

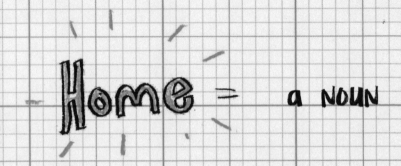

Home = a NOUN

A Place
where THERE
is love.

CHAPTER 22

That night, Rosie packed her engineer's stash under the bed as she did every night. She climbed under the covers and looked around her room. She loved her house, but what made it her home were Gizmo and her aunts and uncles, her friends, and her neighbors. And now, the Riveters. They were all her family.

She thought about the Raucous Riveters and Mrs. Lu. They lived in many houses, but their home was really anywhere they were together.

They were amazing women, and Rosie was proud to know them and even prouder to be an honorary Riveter.

Rosie made a final note in her engineer's journal.

She wished Gizmo good night. Tired but very happy, Rosie Revere drifted to sleep and dreamed the bold dreams of a great engineer.

PaiNTaPalooZa 6: WRETCHed WRECK
PaiNTaPalooZa 7: MeSSY MiSadVENTURe
PaiNTaPalooZa 8: FOOlhaRdY FlOP
PaiNTaPalooZa 9: ~~DORKY Dud~~
~~FUTile FiaSCO~~
A HaPPY HOMECOMiNg!

TOILET FILL VALVE

HEART VALVE

TIRE VALVE

ODE TO A VALVE

What is a valve?
What does it do?

It's simply a gate
that lets fluids go through

a tube or a hose
or a pipe or a vein,

and keeps them from flowing
backward again.

There are valves in your toilet.
Valves in your heart.

Valves in your tires,
and that's just a start.

So pooh-pooh to those who say,
"No need to gush!"

Instead say "Hooray!"
the next time that you flush.

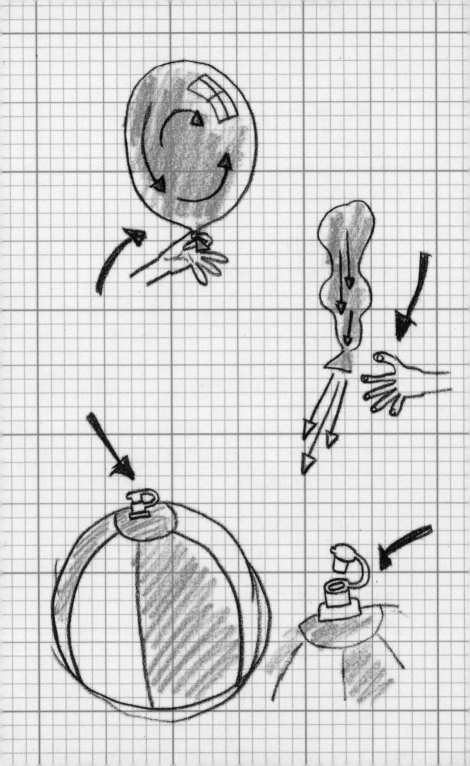

ABOUT VALVES

If you blow up a balloon and then let go, the air inside the balloon will come out. If you blow up a beach ball and then let go, the air inside will *not* come out. Why not? A tiny flap of plastic inside the beach ball blocks the hole and keeps the air contained. This mechanism is a very simple *valve*.

There are many kinds of valves, but they all do the same thing: They control the flow of liquid or gas through a tube or pipe. When you turn on the faucet, a valve opens and lets water flow through. Your stove and grill have valves that control the release of gas to the burners.

Even your toilet has valves that let water fill the tank so you can flush when you need to. That is important!

Are there valves in your bike? Car? A trumpet? What about in your body?

The answer is yes! Your body has over fifty valves that keep fluids flowing in the right direction! Some valves in your body are rings of muscles that contract. Others are flaps of tissue that block blood from flowing backward into your heart. Be glad you have valves!

ABOUT THE RIVETERS

During World War II, millions of women in the United States, the United Kingdom, Australia, Canada, New Zealand, and other allied nations worked to provide the food and equipment needed for the war effort. Some worked on farms. Others worked in businesses and factories. In the United States, these factory-working women were represented by Rosie the Riveter, the scarf-wearing character whose slogan was "We can do it!"

Riveters used metal rods to connect sheets of metal. Riveters and other workers built ships, airplanes, tanks, and jeeps. They also made guns and bullets. American factories were open every day and every night, and the workers made more than three hundred thousand aircraft, eighty-six thousand tanks, and two million army trucks during World War II!

Women began working in the war production factories after many men left to fight in Europe, Africa, and Asia. The jobs paid well. Eighteen million women worked in the U.S. war effort. Most of these women were poor and held low-paying jobs before the war. About six million of these women were housewives who had not worked outside the home before. Having so many women at work in industry and production was a big change for America.

Factory work was difficult and dangerous. Women were paid less than the men who had worked the same jobs, and women of color were paid even less than white women. They also faced racism on the job and were often given more dangerous tasks.

The hard work of the Riveters helped the Allies win World War II. When the war ended, many factories closed. Others gave the women's jobs back to men after the men came home from the war. Even so, America now knew that women could do all kinds of jobs.

Rosie the Riveter and her real-life counterparts made a big difference during the war and helped to shape the civil rights movement and the continuing fight for equal rights for women that followed.

GREAT-GREAT-AUNT ROSE

BERNICE

MADE AIRPLANES
a LONG TIME ago!

TRAVELED all AROUND
THE WORLD!

BOSS

WAS BORN IN a
DIFFERENT COUNTRY!

THINK ABOUT THIS

Think of all the things you have done in your life. Now can you imagine all you will do by the time you are as old as Great-Great-Aunt Rose, Bernice, or Boss? You will have so many interesting stories to tell.

Think about the older people in your life and in your town. Take time to ask them about their stories. Who knows—maybe one of them was a Rosie the Riveter or knew someone who was!

ABOUT THE AUTHOR

ANDREA BEATY is the bestselling author of *Rosie Revere, Engineer*; *Ada Twist, Scientist*; and *Iggy Peck, Architect*; as well as the novels *Dorko the Magnificent* and *Attack of the Fluffy Bunnies*. She has a degree in biology and computer science and spent many years in the computer industry. She now writes children's books in her home outside Chicago.

ABOUT THE ILLUSTRATOR

DAVID ROBERTS has illustrated many books, including *Rosie Revere, Engineer*; *Ada Twist, Scientist*; *Iggy Peck, Architect*; and *Happy Birthday, Madame Chapeau*. He lives in London, where, when not drawing, he likes to make hats.

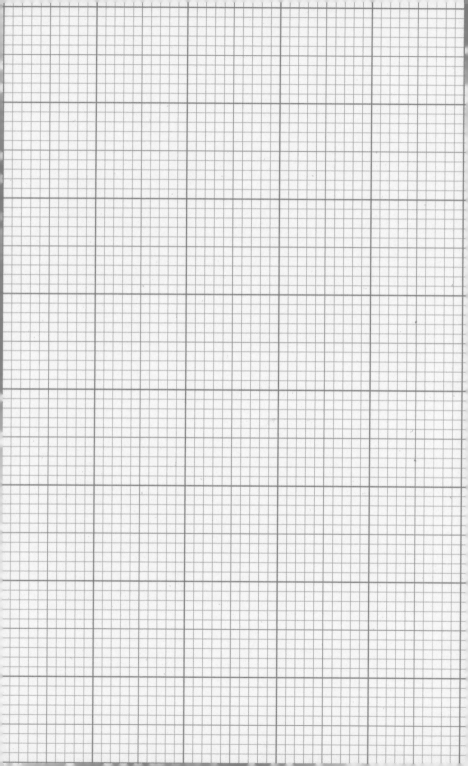

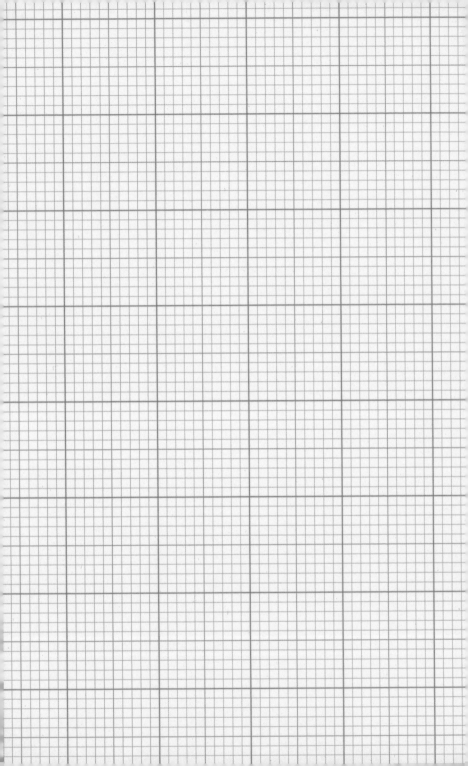